THE CLASH OF THE CREEPERS

THE CLASH OF THE CREEPERS

AN UNOFFICIAL GAMER'S ADVENTURE
BOOK SIX

Winter Morgan

Sky Pony Press
New York

Sky Pony Press books may be purchased in bulk at special discounts for sales promotion, corporate gifts, fund-raising, or educational purposes. Special editions can also be created to specifications. For details, contact the Special Sales Department, Sky Pony Press, 307 West 36th Street, 11th Floor, New York, NY 10018 or info@skyhorsepublishing.com.

Visit our website at www.skyponypress.com.

10 9 8 7 6 5 4 3 2 1

Library of Congress Cataloging-in-Publication Data is available on file.

Cover photo by Megan Miller

Print ISBN: 978-1-63450-591-8
Ebook ISBN: 978-1-63450-592-5

Printed in Canada

TABLE OF CONTENTS

THE CLASH OF THE CREEPERS

Chapter 1
BORROWED MAP

Steve was hard at work on a new irrigation system for his wheat farm when he saw familiar faces in the distance.

"Steve," Lucy called out, as she sprinted across the field toward him.

His friends Henry and Max raced behind Lucy.

"I didn't know you guys were in town," Steve said. He was happy to see his old friends.

"We aren't staying," Henry told Steve. "We just came to pick you up and take you on a treasure hunt."

"That's nice of you but I think I'd like to stick around the farm. I'm working on a new irrigation system. My crops aren't growing and I think they need more water." Steve stood by a patch of carrots that were in desperate need of irrigation.

"That can wait," demanded Lucy. "We heard about a magical mountain that contains endless diamonds, and we want you to come find it with us."

"How do you know it even exists?" questioned Steve.

"We don't, but we're going to find out," replied Henry.

"I don't think I'm going to leave my farm to travel through the Overworld in hopes of finding a mountain that you aren't even sure exists." Steve was annoyed.

"But you have to come with us," pleaded Lucy. "You're so resourceful and such a skilled fighter."

"You have Max, he's the fighter." Steve went back to working on his irrigation system.

Max walked over to Steve and showed him a map. "Look. This adventure map has the mountain on it. According to the map, the mountain is past the jungle and by the ocean biome. We've traveled through all of those biomes before, and we know how to survive in them. This is a no-brainer! We have to make this trip."

"How did you get that map?" asked Steve.

"We were treasure hunting when we stumbled upon a group of explorers. We wound up mining with them, and one of the explorers started to talk about the mountain. Apparently they had been there and it was amazing. It has countless diamonds." Lucy was so excited she rushed the words out in one breath.

"And they gave you the map?" Steve was curious. After being attacked by griefers in the past, he didn't trust anybody not in his circle of friends. How did his friends know this wasn't a trick? That a griefer gave them a fake map leading them to a trap?

"Well, they didn't give it to us," Max fumbled with his words.

"Did you steal it?" Steve couldn't believe his ears. These were his good friends, and he knew they weren't thieves.

"Let's just say we borrowed it," Henry said and smiled.

"You stole it!" Steve raised his voice, "How could you do something like that?"

"It's not as bad as you think," explained Lucy. "They dropped it when they were destroyed by a creeper. We escaped, but I was able to pick up the map."

"But this isn't our map," said Steve.

Lucy defended herself, "I do want to find them and give the map back."

"Yes, we just want to do it after we get the diamonds," Henry said as he looked over Max's shoulder and studied the map.

"And the group had already been to the mountain and mined for diamonds. They were only keeping the map so they could return when they needed more," Lucy told Steve.

Steve wasn't sure what to make of his friends' proposal. He needed to work on his irrigation system, but he also wanted to go on an adventure with his friends. Steve's one serious issue with the trip was he didn't trust the map.

"Are you sure they didn't drop it on purpose? Maybe they wanted you to take it and once we get to the mountain they will trap us. Maybe your new friends are griefers," Steve guessed.

"Well, there is only one way to find out," said Max.

"If it is a trap, we can fight the evil griefers and save others from the same fate," Lucy reasoned with Steve. She knew that he loved to stop griefers from terrorizing innocent people.

The sun was setting. Steve looked at his friends and warned, "We need to get back to my house before hostile mobs start spawning."

The gang heard a shrill scream coming from his neighbor Kyra's house.

"Oh no! It sounds like Kyra is being attacked. We have to help her," Steve shouted to his friends. They sprinted toward Kyra's house.

As they approached the house, they could see through the window that Kyra was battling four zombies with her diamond sword, while more vacant-eyed zombies lumbered toward her.

"Help!" Kyra screamed as she destroyed two zombies with her sword.

Max shot an arrow at a zombie. The others charged at the undead creatures, striking them with their swords.

"Good, we destroyed them! Quick, come inside my house before more zombies spawn," yelled Kyra.

Steve looked around and didn't see any zombies. Everyone ran inside Kyra's house. Steve lit a torch and placed it on the door outside the house to protect them from hostile mobs. He also placed another torch on the wall inside.

"Oh Steve," Kyra smiled, "you're always thinking ahead."

"You know me," Steve blushed.

"Lucy, Max, and Henry," Kyra remarked, "I had no idea you guys were in town."

"We're not staying very long. We want to search for a magical mountain that has an endless supply of diamonds," Lucy told her.

"Mine Mountain!" exclaimed Kyra. "I've heard about it. I didn't know it really existed. I thought it was just a myth."

"Well, we have a map." Max showed Kyra the map.

"Wow! Can I come with you?" asked Kyra.

"Of course. We were planning on coming over here and asking you," Lucy told her friend.

"Are you going, Steve?" Kyra questioned as she stared at the map.

"I wasn't planning on it, but now I think I'll go. Truthfully Kyra, I don't trust this map. I think it's a trick and someone is trying to trap us, and I want to be there for you guys if something goes wrong," said Steve.

"Oh Steve, you are always worried about something. Can't you just be excited for our adventure?" Kyra asked her friend.

"After all our run-ins with griefers," replied Steve, "I just want to be cautious."

"I understand. But if this isn't a trick, we can actually go to Mine Mountain. I've heard there are so many diamonds, the mine is filled with a blue glow." Kyra couldn't believe her friends had a map to this mythical place.

"We should get some sleep before we head on our journey to the mountain," Steve suggested to them.

"Great!" Max said as he climbed into a bed at Kyra's and snuggled underneath the red wool blanket.

Kaboom!

"That sounds like it was coming from my house," Steve hollered as he jumped out of bed. "I guess we aren't going to get any sleep tonight."

Chapter 2
TREASURE HUNT

As Steve and his friends sprinted in the dark, an arrow struck Kyra.

"Ouch!" screamed Kyra.

"Look, skeletons!" Max pointed out two white bony creatures behind a tree.

"I've been hit, too!" exclaimed Lucy. "It's so dark, I can't see. Where are they?" She took out her bow and arrow.

Max shot an arrow at the skeletons. "Can't you see them? Behind that tree?"

Max hit the skeleton. Henry charged at the bony beast with his diamond sword. Steve followed. They used all of their might to defeat the skeletons.

Click! Clack! Clang! The sound of bones rattled as the skeletons lost their battle to Steve and his friends.

"We need to get to my house," instructed Steve. "I need to see what has been destroyed."

As Max ran toward the house, he fell into a hole. "Oh no!" he shouted, "Help me!"

Steve had a ladder near his house and gave it to Max. Max slowly climbed up the ladder in the dark and made his way safely out of the hole.

"I guess this was where the explosion occurred," Henry noted, looking at the hole.

"Looks like a skeleton destroyed a creeper," Lucy said as she picked up a CD.

"Thankfully, it was outside the wheat farm. I just couldn't deal with any more damage to the farm," said Steve. He was relieved his farm was intact.

"When a skeleton kills a creeper, that wouldn't leave an explosion," said Max. "This hole looks like it was created by TNT. It definitely is the work of a griefer. Also, skeletons can only shoot at people. There must have been someone else over here."

Steve looked down and saw a piece of wool on the ground. "Do you think Thomas is back to his old ways?"

"I don't know," remarked Kyra, "but we better be on the lookout for Thomas or any other griefers."

"Look out!" Henry screamed as he saw a green creeper approaching the wheat farm.

Max aimed his bow and arrow toward the creeper. He was about to shoot when Snuggles and Jasmine appeared. Both ocelots meowed and the creeper left the wheat farm.

"Snuggles and Jasmine saved the day," Steve said as he walked over to his two pet felines.

"I had the creeper in sight. I could have destroyed it," said Max.

"We've had enough explosions for one day," Steve told his friend.

The sun began to rise. "Ugh, there's no time to sleep now." Max was annoyed. "We should get ready for our trip to Mine Mountain."

"I'll hunt for breakfast," remarked Lucy, and she left the group, armed with a bow and arrow.

Steve walked into his house and opened a large chest that sat in the corner of his living room.

"We're going to need a lot of supplies for this trip. I studied the map and it isn't an easy journey." Steve looked through the chest, took out his most powerful diamond armor, swords, and bows and arrows, and placed them in his inventory.

"Do you have any potions?" asked Henry. "I'm running low and I think some might come in handy."

Steve agreed and placed potions of invisibility, underwater breathing, fire resistance, and many others into his inventory. "Wow, when I come back, I will be seriously low on supplies," Steve told his friends.

"We'll help you replenish your stock," Kyra reassured him cheerfully. "Once we reach Mine Mountain, we'll have so many diamonds that we can trade them for all the supplies in the Overworld."

Lucy walked into the living room and announced, "I broiled a chicken. You should come outside and eat before we start our journey. We want to have full health and food bars."

The group gathered on the grass outside of Steve's house and dined on chicken and apples.

"How long do you think it will take us to reach Mine Mountain?" asked Kyra, as she took a bite of the juicy chicken.

Max gazed at the map, calculating distance. "I would estimate two days but you never know what might slow us down."

Henry looked over the map and asked, "But don't we want to stop at that jungle temple first and unearth the treasure?"

"Ah, yes," Max replied as he looked at the map and noted the jungle temple. "We can get to that temple by the end of the day."

The group was excited for their journey. As they finished the last bit of chicken, a bunny hopped by them. Max took out his bow and arrow.

"You don't have to shoot it," Lucy told him. "We already ate chicken. We don't need rabbit stew."

"I don't trust this rabbit," Max said, staring at the furry white rabbit.

"But bunnies are peaceful," declared Kyra as she approached the bunny with a carrot.

"Stop!" screamed Max. "Look at those evil red eyes!"

Baring its large teeth, the bunny leapt at Kyra.

"Oh no!" Steve grabbed his bow and arrow. "Kyra!"

Kyra struck the rabbit with her diamond sword; it retreated but then rushed toward her, ready to attack.

Max and Steve shot arrows at the small killer rabbit. However Lucy charged at the rabbit with a nametag.

"What are you doing?" asked Kyra in a rather loud voice.

"Are you crazy?" Max was shocked at Lucy's behavior.

Lucy grabbed the evil bunny and placed a nametag that read Toast around the bunny's neck. The bunny transformed into a docile bunny, its white fur turned to patches of black and white.

"How can you call me crazy, Max? That's not nice at all." Lucy fed the calm bunny a carrot.

"But how did you do that?" Max stood by the bunny and put down his bow and arrow. He was in shock.

"If you change the name to Toast, it calms the bunny down," Lucy said, as if charging at a feral bunny and placing a nametag on the animal were the easiest thing in the world.

"Wow, I'm impressed," declared Steve.

The group gazed in wonderment at the bunny while they gathered all of their supplies for the journey. They walked through the town, making sure to visit their friend Eliot the Blacksmith before they set out on their adventure.

Eliot was always happy to see his friends. He smiled as they walked through the door of his shop.

"How are you guys doing? Need to trade anything?" he asked them.

Steve took out some wheat from his inventory. "I'd like to trade this wheat. I need some emeralds."

"Are your friends here to help you build that irrigation system on your farm?"

"No, we need the emeralds because we are about to go to Mine Mountain, and we need as many resources as we can carry. It's going to be a long journey," Steve told Eliot.

"Wow, Mine Mountain. I didn't even think that place really existed." Eliot said. He took Steve's wheat and gave him a handful of emeralds.

"Well, we will find out for ourselves if it really exists," Steve exclaimed as he took the emeralds and placed them in his inventory.

"How exciting! When you come back, you need to tell me all about it!" Eliot waved goodbye to the group.

"Okay, Steve. Let's go," said Henry.

"Wait," Steve replied and walked toward the library. "I have to get books from Avery the Librarian."

"Books?" Max was shocked. "Why?"

"I want to trade these emeralds so I can get all the books about Mine Mountain. I think they might come in handy."

"That's Steve. Always thinking," Lucy smiled.

Steve walked into the library and Avery greeted him. "Steve, are you going somewhere?"

"Yes. I am going to find Mine Mountain," Steve told Avery. "Do you have any books about it?"

"Of course." Avery led Steve over to a shelf with a stack of leather-bound books. "Here they are."

Steve picked up three books and offered, "I'd like to trade some emeralds for the books."

"Okay, Steve. But you must promise to come back here once you return. I've only read about Mine Mountain in books, and I'd love to hear about it from a person who has actually found it." Avery thanked Steve for the emeralds.

Steve placed the books in his inventory and joined his friends. As the group walked past the town and into the thick of the tree-filled jungle, Steve hoped he'd have diamonds to trade with Eliot when he returned. He took a deep breath. He wanted to see the famed Mine Mountain, but there was still a part of him that believed it didn't exist—and they were heading into a trap.

Chapter 3
SIMILAR PLANS

The group stayed on the narrow path through the lush jungle.

"The map says the temple is here." Max pointed to the right.

"It must be hidden behind the leaves," remarked Henry.

Steve sheared the leaves where Max said the temple should be located, but there wasn't anything hidden behind the leaves. "I told you this map was a hoax!"

Max silently studied the map.

"Max, are you sure it's to the right?" asked Henry.

Max continued to look at the map and didn't comment.

Henry walked on the path Steve had sheared. He looked through the leaves shading the path and noted, "I think I see something."

The group followed Henry. Very far in the distance, they could make out a moss stone structure that looked like a jungle temple.

"I knew it!" exclaimed Max. "The map was right, it just seems to be slightly off with the location. It appears that the jungle temple looks a lot closer on this map."

Steve sheared a clear path toward the temple. As they got closer they could see the entrance.

"It's definitely a jungle temple," Lucy said enthusiastically. "I just hope the treasure is still there. I hope somebody didn't get to it first."

"Shh!" warned Kyra, then with a whisper she asked the group, "Do you guys hear voices?"

The gang paused. They could hear people talking.

"Yes," whispered Lucy, "I hope it isn't griefers."

The group looked for rainbow griefers but they didn't see any.

"Look straight ahead." Max pointed at two people who wore matching blue helmets walking toward the jungle temple.

"Shh!" said Lucy, but it was too late.

Max's loud voice had captured the attention of the two people who stood by the temple.

"Who are you?" asked one of the blue-helmeted people.

"We could ask you the same question!" Steve's voice boomed back.

"I have nothing to hide. My name is Beatrice, and this is Charlie," Beatrice called as she walked toward them.

Max noticed Charlie also had a map in his hand. "Where did you get that map?"

"None of your business!" proclaimed Charlie.

"It looks similar to the map I have." Max paused for a moment, then continued, "Did your map make the temple appear closer than it is? Is the map's scale a bit off?"

"Yes!" Charlie was surprised and responded, "Why?"

"Maybe you were right, Steve," said Max. "Maybe this is a trick."

"What's a trick?" questioned Beatrice.

"Would you mind telling us where you got that map?" asked Max.

"We can tell them," Beatrice told her friend.

Charlie replied, "We were given the map by a very nice group of explorers."

"Did they call themselves the Exciting Explorers?" asked Max.

"Yes!" exclaimed Beatrice.

"I told you not to trust that map," remarked Steve.

"What are you guys talking about?" Beatrice was confused. "They were very nice people, and they said they couldn't get to this treasure so they offered us the map."

"They didn't just give us the map," added Charlie, "we traded them two diamonds and an emerald for it."

"For a map that could be fake?" Max asked them.

"Why? What did you trade them for the map?"

Max didn't reply. He simply said, "I guess we should enter the temple and see if it's a trap."

The group headed toward the temple. There were no griefers in sight as they walked downstairs in the direction of the treasure. They stepped around the tripwire and took out their pickaxes to unearth the treasure chest.

"I think we just have to pull this lever," said Charlie.

"NO!" Max shouted.

But it was too late. Charlie pulled the lever and an arrow shot through the air.

"I've been hit," cried Lucy.

Charlie apologized, "I didn't realize. I'm sorry. I'm a builder, not a treasure hunter."

"Well, we're expert treasure hunters, so you should listen to us," Henry told him.

"Henry, be nice," chastised Lucy.

"Look what I found," Henry said with a smile. Two large chests were in sight.

"Open them!" Kyra called out.

"Yes! Let's see what's inside!" Charlie walked closer to the chest.

Beatrice approached the first chest and accidentally stepped on the tripwire.

Kaboom! There was a loud TNT explosion.

"Is everyone okay?" Steve called out.

There was silence.

Chapter 4
FACT OR FABLE?

"Are you guys okay?" Steve asked again.

"I'm fine," Max called out.

Steve let out a sigh of relief when he heard from the others. But there were two people missing. Charlie and Beatrice were gone.

Lucy spoke quickly, "Oh my! The TNT destroyed them! How awful. I wonder where they will respawn?"

"That's not the only thing that's missing!" Henry pointed to the treasure. The two chests had also gone up in a puff of smoke.

"How did they do that?" asked Steve.

"I have no idea," Henry said. He was dumbfounded.

"I knew we shouldn't have trusted them," Steve complained while he paced.

Max searched through his inventory. "The map! They took our map to Mine Mountain!"

"What? How?" Steve couldn't believe his ears.

"Clearly they are extremely skilled thieves," proclaimed Henry.

"There's only one thing we can do. We must find them and get our map back," Steve told the gang.

"And we also have to kill that skeleton!" Lucy pointed to a skeleton walking down the stairs.

Click. Clang. The skeleton took out its bow and arrow and aimed at Steve.

Max ran toward the skeleton and destroyed it with one strike.

"Good job, Max," Lucy commended him.

"We have to get out of here." Henry had a worried tone to his voice as he noticed a brick of TNT in the corner. "I don't trust Charlie and Beatrice. They could have placed TNT all over this temple. We have to get out fast."

The gang surged toward the door and into the jungle. They didn't have a map but they knew they had to get far away from the temple.

"I see a village in the distance," Kyra pointed out to the others.

Steve could see sheep and a horse in the field near some shops. "Yes, I see it! Let's go that way."

The group walked on the yellow grass and into the gravel-filled streets of the village.

"Should we go into the butcher shop?" asked Lucy. "I think we need some food."

"No, my health bar is okay. Your chicken really filled me up," replied Henry.

Steve saw a familiar face walking into the library. He ran toward the door.

"Steve!" His old friend Adam called out. "What are you doing here?"

"I'm here with Max, Lucy, Henry, and Kyra. We are on an adventure."

"Sounds like fun," Adam replied.

Henry and the others, excited to see their old friend, walked into the library.

"Shhh!" the librarian warned them. "You have to be quiet in the library."

"Let's go outside," suggested Adam, afraid of angering the librarian.

The sun was setting outside the library, so Adam invited his friends to stay at his house for the night.

"When did you move to this village?" asked Steve.

"Just recently. I found it when I was collecting resources to make potions and I stumbled upon this village. Everyone was so friendly, I decided to stay," explained Adam.

"Where's Thomas?" asked Steve.

"Funny you should ask about him. I heard he was back in your old town," replied Adam.

Steve paused. He remembered the piece of wool he had seen by his wheat farm. He hoped Thomas wasn't back to his old shenanigans and planning on destroying Steve's wheat farm, or even the town. Steve almost wanted to give up and head back home to make sure everything was okay. Of course he wanted to see Mine Mountain, but he also didn't want all of his hard work destroyed while he was off trying to find a place that might not even exist.

"Guys," Steve said to his friends, "now that we have lost our map, maybe we should go home."

"Go home? No, we will find it! Don't worry." Henry tried to convince Steve they should continue on their journey, but Steve didn't want to hear any of it.

Adam interrupted, "What map? What are you talking about?"

"We were headed to Mine Mountain. We had a map," explained Lucy.

Adam walked over to a chest that sat next to the fireplace in his modest home. He opened the chest and took out a map. "Is this the same map you had?"

Max took the map from Adam's hands and studied it. Max nodded his head. "Yes, this is it. Where did you get it?"

"A while ago some explorers came to town, and they traded the map for some potions. I've always wanted to go to Mine Mountain, but I didn't think I could make the trip alone." Adam looked over Max's shoulders at the map.

"Well, you're not going to do it alone," Lucy told him, "you're going to come with us."

"Really?" Adam said excitedly, "You want me to come with you?"

"Yes," said Steve, "we'll leave in the morning."

Adam was thrilled. "I can't believe I'm finally going to make this trip."

The only person who wasn't excited was Steve. As the group climbed into their beds, Steve thought about Thomas and the damage he might be doing to Steve's town. He realized that they had to make it to Mine Mountain. Steve would need all the diamonds he could fit into his inventory to rebuild his town. As he drifted off to sleep, he imagined Thomas blowing up the shops and the houses.

Steve didn't sleep very long. There was a noise coming from the living room; it sounded like someone was at the door.

"Don't move," Steve told the others, as he put on his diamond armor. "I'm going to see who or what is at the door."

Steve walked through Adam's living room. He could make out a vacant-eyed zombie ripping the hinges off the wooden door.

"Get ready to battle!" Steve called out to his friends.

The gang put on their armor and rushed toward the door. Steve struck the zombie with his diamond sword, destroying it. Outside there were more zombies walking toward Adam's house.

Max shot arrows at the zombies, while the others charged toward them. It seemed as if there were a never-ending army of zombies. Steve and his friends wondered if they'd lose the battle.

"If only the sun would come up now," Steve said as he struck a zombie.

"I don't think that's going to happen," replied Henry as he clobbered two zombies.

"Look, somebody is helping us," Lucy noted when a sea of arrows flew in the direction of the zombies. The arrows hit a group of the terrors of the night and they were destroyed.

Two people wearing red helmets sprinted toward Steve and his friends and helped them battle the menacing zombies.

"Who are you?" Kyra asked as they destroyed the last few zombies together.

"I'm Owen and this is my friend, Cyrus."

"They're my neighbors," clarified Adam.

The sun began to rise. Lucy suggested, "Please join us for breakfast. You were so nice to help us."

"The zombies were attacking everyone. We were just protecting the town. There is no need to thank us," replied Cyrus.

"I insist," said Lucy.

The group feasted on apples and potatoes from Adam's small farm.

"Can you look after my house?" Adam asked his neighbors Owen and Cyrus, "I'm leaving with my friends soon and we won't be back for a while."

"Where are you going?" questioned Cyrus.

"We're going to Mine Mountain," Lucy told them.

"We've been planning a trip there, too. We were supposed to go with our friends, Charlie and Beatrice. They had a map and everything," said Cyrus.

Lucy was silent. Could she be hearing them right? Charlie and Beatrice were the treasure thieves.

"You should join us," said Steve as he looked at his group, "maybe you will find your friends there."

Steve's friends were shocked that he invited Charlie and Beatrice's friends. Steve wished he could convey to his friends that he hoped Cyrus and Owen might lead them to Charlie and Beatrice and then Steve would be able to find out why they stole the treasure. Also Steve knew it was a good idea to keep potential enemies close by so you could keep an eye on them.

"Do you guys have a map?" asked Cyrus.

"Yes, we have everything necessary for a journey like this," said Henry.

The group gathered together their resources for the trip. Afterward, they stood around Adam's map, plotting the journey.

"It looks like we have to travel through the swamp," Max pointed out.

"I hope we don't get attacked by slimes," said Lucy fervently.

They could see the swampy land in the horizon. They were on their way.

Chapter 5
WARRIORS AND WITCHES

Night was setting in as they approached the swamp. As the light of the day grew fainter, a full moon appeared, filling the night sky with a dim glow.

"We need to find shelter." Steve looked around and began to construct a crude structure.

Kyra grabbed some wooden planks to help Steve with the house. "If we all pitch in and start building, we'll be able to finish the house quickly and we can stay safe."

The others grabbed what they could to help with the construction of the house. A bat whizzed by, almost flying into Steve.

"That's not a good sign," Steve said as he looked up. "I think one of us should keep watch for hostile mobs. I know when I see a bat, I usually see a witch."

"Don't worry, Steve," Adam consoled. He lit a torch and looked around. "It looks like there isn't any evil brewing around here. Just concentrate on the house."

The group worked as fast as they could, gathering every resource they had to build the house.

"Wow, I can't believe how quickly we can build a house if we all work together," Lucy remarked as she grabbed another wooden plank.

"I know!" Kyra was amazed, too. "We can finally get some sleep."

Cyrus placed the door on the house and Owen began to craft beds with wool and wood planks.

"Come inside," said Owen, "the beds are almost ready."

Steve and his friends placed the final wooden planks and the house was finished. Everyone raced inside.

"Where's Adam?" asked Steve as he climbed into bed.

The gang glanced over at the empty bed.

"I think he's still outside," replied Cyrus, "I'll go look for him."

Steve followed Cyrus outside to search for Adam.

"I don't see him." Cyrus looked around and began to feel nervous. "I think we should put on some armor. It's not good to be out here without it."

Cyrus and Steve put on their diamond armor, although Cyrus still wore his red leather helmet. They trekked deep into the swamp biome, walking along a stream of murky shallow water lined with lily pads. Another bat flew close to Steve's head.

"Where is Adam?" Cyrus was getting worried. "How far could he have gone?"

"I hope he wasn't destroyed. He'd respawn at his house and never get to Mine Mountain with us. And he really wanted to go." Steve thought about Adam.

He wondered what hostile mob might have attacked him or if he had simply gone too far and gotten lost.

"Help!" a voice called out.

"That sounds like Adam!" yelled Cyrus.

"Look!" Steve pointed and exclaimed, "a witch hut!"

Steve and Cyrus jogged toward the witch hut. They could see the witch throw a potion on Adam and he appeared to move quite slowly. Steve rushed toward the witch and struck her with his diamond sword. The witch splashed the remainder of her potion on Steve.

"I'm very weak!" Adam called out to Cyrus. Adam stood close to the witch and didn't move.

"Run, Adam!" shouted Cyrus, but Adam stood motionless.

Cyrus shot an arrow at the witch but the purple-robed witch drank a potion and regained her strength as she grabbed another vile of her potent potion and aimed it at Adam. The drops from the potion of poison almost fell on Adam, when Cyrus sprinted toward the witch, striking her with his diamond sword. She was weakened. Steve used what little energy he had to deliver the final blow. The witch was destroyed, dropping sugarcane. Steve picked it up.

"Adam, are you okay?" asked Steve.

Cyrus gave him a potion of healing, which he drank very quickly.

"Thanks guys. You saved me. I'm feeling much better now."

Cyrus looked at the witch hut. "I hope there aren't any more witches in that hut. I think we have to get back to the house. We need to be safe and rest up for our trip."

They all agreed and raced back to the house. The house was in sight when they heard a noise.

Boing! Boing! Boing!

"What's that?" asked Cyrus.

"It sounds like slimes but I don't see any." Steve could hear the slimes bouncing. He searched through the moss-covered trees and the sugarcane that lined the swamp's water.

"They're over there!" Cyrus shouted as four large green slimes bounced toward them.

Adam ran toward the slimes, striking two with his sword. The two slimes broke into four smaller slimes.

Cyrus and Steve hit the smaller slimes with their swords, destroying them and leaving small slime balls.

The trio lunged toward the remaining two blocks of green slime, striking them with their swords, and then defeating the smaller slimes.

"Finally, we can head back to the house," Steve said as he walked toward the front door.

"But look at the sky," Cyrus frowned, "it's too late to sleep."

The sun was rising. Their friends were getting up from their slumber. The three of them drank potions to replenish their health bar. "Eventually, I'll get some sleep," Steve said hopefully.

Lucy walked into the living room and greeted her friends, "Were you guys up all night fighting mobs?"

"Yes," Steve replied.

"Wow, I'm impressed. You guys are real warriors," remarked Lucy. "Did you get any rewards from the mobs?"

"The witch dropped sugarcane and the slimes left slime balls," said Steve, as their other friends walked into the small living room.

"You guys fought a witch and a slime? Wow! And all I did was sleep," said Owen.

Everyone agreed that Steve, Cyrus, and Adam deserved a big breakfast. As they ate, Max studied the map.

"Well, it's time for us to move on." Max looked at the map as he spoke.

"Which way do we go?" asked Lucy.

"Toward the forest," Max said, as they started off into the forest filled with oak and birch trees, and wolves.

Chapter 6
NETHER AGAIN

"The forest is so pretty!" Lucy remarked as she looked at the green leaves and watched cows graze in the pasture.

"Mine Mountain is just beyond the forest. According to the map, it's not that far." Max stared at the map and said optimistically, "I think we can get there before nightfall."

"Really? I hope so!" Kyra was excited.

Boom!

"What's that noise?" Owen asked with a shaky voice.

Rain fell as Max replied, "Thunder."

The sky grew thick with clouds and the sun was hidden, making it the perfect environment for hostile mobs. Two skeletons emerged from behind an oak tree and shot arrows at the group.

"Oh no!" Lucy's arm was hit. She grabbed her bow and arrow with her good arm and aimed at the skeletons.

The gang ran toward the skeletons, striking them with their diamond swords. No matter how many they destroyed, more would spawn and replace them.

"Zombies!" Cyrus called out.

The group fought the skeletons as an army of zombies lumbered toward them.

"I have an idea!" Steve began to craft a portal.

"Yes! The Nether!" Adam was excited.

"I've never met someone who was excited for a trip to the Nether," remarked Owen.

"I need to replenish my supplies to make potions. I can brew a lot with Nether wart."

"This is no time to talk!" shouted Steve.

Adam struck a skeleton with his sword.

"Good, keep fighting!" Steve instructed the group. "I'll build the portal."

Steve ignited the Nether portal and purple mist filled the rainy skies.

"Come on guys!" Steve shouted to his friends. "We have to stand on the portal now or we'll be trapped in this rainy forest filled with hostile mobs."

The gang rushed toward the portal, but Kyra was cornered by two skeletons and a trio of zombies and couldn't join the others. "Help!" she screamed as the zombies attacked her.

The gang was on the portal; within seconds they would travel to the Nether.

"What should we do?" asked a panicked Owen. "We have to help Kyra."

"Don't get off the portal," demanded Steve, "I'll help Kyra."

Steve got out of the portal as the others vanished. He sprinted toward Kyra with his diamond sword.

"Don't worry, Steve," voices called out from behind him. Max and Henry had also jumped out of the portal.

As much as Steve didn't want to admit it, he was happy he had backup. The three friends raced to Kyra's side, saving her from the zombies and skeletons. But the battle was still intense and everyone's health bar was getting low.

"We'll never win this battle!" Steve told them, "Can you guys fight them off while I build another portal?"

"We'll try," Kyra shouted as she struck a skeleton and didn't even have time to pick up the dropped bone because a zombie was making its way toward her.

Steve used the last of his obsidian to construct the Nether portal. "This is our last chance. I don't have any more obsidian. We have to go now!"

"We're ready!" Kyra sprinted toward Steve as he ignited the portal. The portal omitted a loud sound as the purple mist filled the air. They were going to be reunited with their friends.

"It's going to be okay," Steve said as they emerged into the red glow of the Nether next to a lava waterfall.

"No, it's not!" Max screamed as a high-pitched sound pierced his ears and a fireball shot at him. Max took out his bow and arrow and shot the fireball. It bounced back and struck the white ghast.

"Good job, Max," Steve commended him as he walked through the Nether looking for their missing friends.

"I wonder where they are?" Henry looked off into the distance and then climbed up a pillar to get a better view of the landscape.

"Do you see them at all?" Kyra asked as she called out their names but got no response.

"No, I don't see anything." Henry was disappointed.

"Look," Max pointed out as he jumped over a pool of lava. "I see a Nether fortress. I bet that's where we'll find our missing friends."

The trio raced toward the Nether fortress. The entrance was in sight when they heard chirping sounds.

"That doesn't sound like a bird." Max looked up in the sky. Three ghasts were flying toward them.

"Get your bows and arrows out," instructed Henry. "I'm no weatherman but I predict in a few seconds there is going to be a fireball storm."

Max shot an arrow at the ghasts. One shot a fireball but the two other ghasts flew away.

"They get scared when they're attacked," Henry said as his arrow struck the fireball and it flew back at the ghasts.

"Quick, let's get into the Nether fortress." Steve ran through the entrance. The main room was empty.

"Maybe they're getting the treasure?" asked Max.

"Lucy! Owen! Cyrus! Adam!" Steve shouted, but there was no response.

"I hope they're here," Kyra said in a worried tone. "What if they were destroyed by ghasts and are in the Overworld?"

"We should at least try and find the treasure, so this trip isn't a total waste," Henry remarked as he searched the fortress for treasure.

Kyra stopped by the edge of the staircase. "Steve, doesn't Nether wart usually grow here?"

Steve looked at the side of the stairs and noticed there wasn't any red Nether wart growing out of the patch of soul sand. "Yes, it does. It looks like somebody already picked the Nether wart."

"I bet it was Adam! He needed the Nether wart to make potions." Kyra hoped that her friends were in the fortress.

Henry turned a corner and yelled, "Ouch!" A wither skeleton struck Henry with his stone sword, infecting him with the wither.

"Don't worry, it only lasts ten seconds," Steve called out to his friend.

Max struck the black stone carrying a wither skeleton, destroying it. The wither skeleton dropped a skull.

"Awesome!" Max picked up the skull.

Henry was still feeling the effects of the wither.

"Are you okay?" asked Steve.

"I'm not sure. I feel a little funny." Henry's health bar was still diminishing.

"Take this potion," Max said and handed his friend a potion to regain his strength.

"Potion? Did somebody say potion?" Adam asked as he entered the room with the others.

"Have you guys discovered the treasure?" asked Henry.

"No, I think this place was looted before we got here," replied Cyrus.

"I was able to get a bunch of supplies to brew potions," Adam told them.

"I think we should head back to the Overworld. I want to get out of the Nether. It's so dangerous and there is nothing to be gained by being here." Steve hated the Nether. He only built the portal to escape from the mobs. Now he could make another portal back to the Overworld.

"Do we have enough obsidian to make a portal?" questioned Kyra.

The group paused to check their inventories and see if they had enough obsidian.

"It looks like we have to keep moving!" warned Henry.

The group looked up.

"Oh no!" shouted Lucy.

Five yellow blazes flew into the room. Their movements were so gentle they looked as if they were floating in water. The blazes began to catch fire and then each blaze shot three fireballs at the group, surrounding the gang in a sea of flames.

Chapter 7
BLAZE OF GLORY

"I have snowballs!" Max called to his friends, and he tossed as many as he could at the hostile mobs.

"Me too!" Kyra told them and handed out snowballs to her friends. But they didn't have enough snowballs to defeat the flaming mobs.

"We need to find the spawner." Cyrus sprinted toward a blaze with a snowball, knocking it to the ground, and then raced down the hall searching for the room.

The others threw snowballs at the fireballs and shot arrows at the menacing blazes.

"I found the spawner!" Cyrus called out.

"Good, because we're out of snowballs!" cried Max.

"It's over," Henry lamented. "There's no way we can win this, even if Cyrus is able to disarm the spawner."

"Don't give up that quickly," said Steve, "I have a plan."

Max threw his final snowball at the black-eyed flamethrower. "Do you have any more snowballs?"

"No." Steve handed the potion of invisibility to his friends; they all took a gulp and instantly disappeared. The blazes had no idea where their targets were. They couldn't aim fireball at nonexistent people. Everyone rushed toward Cyrus to help him destroy the spawner.

"Cyrus!" Owen called out as he watched his friend unexpectedly get struck with a fireball and disappear.

"Oh no!" cried Lucy.

Adam threw a fire resistant potion at the offending blaze, and Max shot it with an arrow. Henry took this opportunity to reach the spawner and place a bunch of blocks around it. Steve placed torches on the blocks.

"We did it!" Steve called out as the spawner was deactivated.

"But Cyrus is back in the Overworld," Owen said sadly.

"We need to get back to the Overworld too. Did everyone check their obsidian supply?" added Steve.

Together they had enough obsidian to create a portal. The gang headed out of the fortress but stopped when they saw a pair of yellowish eyes hop toward them. The black magma cube jumped at Max.

With a mighty blow from his diamond sword, Henry stopped the cube from attacking his friend. The black cube was similar to the slime and instead of being destroyed, the magma cube morphed into four smaller cubes. The gang struck the smaller cubes. When the cubes were destroyed they dropped magma cream.

Steve picked up the magma cream and handed it to Adam. "Take this cream. You can use it to brew fire resistant potions."

Adam placed the magma cream in his inventory and they rushed out of the fortress. As they walked on the Netherrack ground and looked for a spot to construct a portal to the Overworld, a zombie pigman walked past the group. Since zombie pigmen are usually tame, the group ignored this creature of the Nether, until Steve was using flint and steel and accidentally set an arrow on fire. The flaming arrow flew past the zombie pigman, which began to attack Steve.

More zombie pigmen appeared and began to crowd around the group.

"What should we do?" questioned Lucy when she struck one with her diamond sword, but it didn't seem to hurt the zombie pigman.

"We need to get out of here!" Adam shouted and he gave everyone a potion of swiftness.

The group rushed away from the zombie pigmen and toward a bridge that took them over a large lava river.

"We're safe," Lucy sighed happily.

"But we left the portal. All of our obsidian is over there and now we're trapped in the Nether," Steve said wearily.

"We have to get back to the portal. I want to go to the Overworld and see Cyrus." Owen was upset.

Everyone was exhausted. Steve, Max, and Henry hadn't slept for days, and the battles in the Nether had taken a toll on everyone. Their patience was being tested. A fight began to brew among the friends.

"We need to search for more obsidian," suggested Max.

"Why did we even come to the Nether? This is all your fault, Steve," said Owen.

"This trip to find Mine Mountain has been a nightmare. Who even knows if it really exists?" complained Kyra.

"Stop it!" shouted Steve. He wasn't a fan of raising his voice, but he knew he had to get everyone to pay attention. If they didn't stick together, they'd never get out of the Nether.

"Do you have a plan?" asked Max.

"I can't come up with a plan if everybody is complaining," replied Steve.

The group looked at each other. They knew Steve was right. As they sat silently, they heard voices coming from behind them.

Owen ran a short distance and called out, "Charlie! Beatrice!"

Charlie and Beatrice looked at the others in shock.

"You stole our treasure," Henry exclaimed and pointed his sword at Charlie and Beatrice.

"Stop, Henry. What are you talking about? These are my friends," Owen protested.

"We didn't steal your treasure. We were destroyed. You didn't help save us," said Beatrice.

"Why are you in the Nether?" questioned Steve. He didn't trust this duo and he found it rather suspicious that they had appeared in the Nether.

"We were on a treasure hunt," Charlie replied. "We were just about to go back to the Overworld."

"That's awesome! We need to go back to the Overworld, but we don't have any more obsidian," explained Owen.

"I'm not sure we want to take your new *friends* with us." Charlie looked at Steve as he spoke. "They let us be killed when we were in the jungle temple."

"But you stole the treasure!" cried Henry.

Steve knew Charlie and Beatrice were their only hope of getting back to the Overworld. If they didn't make amends with them, Steve and his friends would be forced to travel to the End to find more obsidian and Steve didn't have enough strength to battle the Ender Dragon. Steve swallowed his pride and apologized. "I'm sorry if we let you down. We didn't want you to get hurt. And I have no idea if you took the treasure or not. We just know that once you disappeared, the treasure and our map were missing. We don't mean any harm. We just need to get back home."

Beatrice looked at Charlie and then she smiled. "Okay, we will let you use our portal."

"Are you going to come with us to Mine Mountain?" asked Owen. "Once we find Cyrus we are going to continue our trip."

Steve was annoyed with Owen. He couldn't believe that Owen trusted these two friends. Steve could tell they were planning something sinister.

"Yes. We'd love to join you," said Beatrice, looking at Owen. "As your friend Steve knows, we were also going to travel to Mine Mountain."

"They say Mine Mountain has enough treasure to supply the entire Overworld with diamonds," proclaimed Owen.

"Great, then there will be enough for everybody," Beatrice said as she placed obsidian and created a portal to the Overworld.

Steve and his friends jumped onto the portal as quickly as they could. They didn't trust Charlie and Beatrice. They could change their minds and leave them in the Nether. The purple mist flew through the air and Steve was excited to return to the Overworld but nervous about what might happen once they got there. *What else would Charlie and Beatrice steal from them?*

Chapter 8

SAFE IN THE SAND

"We're in the desert," said Lucy as she looked around and saw sand.

"Max, take out the map. I want to see where we are and how far we have to travel," said Steve.

Charlie took out his map and asked, "Did you guys get a new map?"

Steve was shocked. *Did Charlie just admit to stealing his map?* "How did you know our map was missing?"

"When we were in the jungle Max dropped the map and I was going to give it back to him. But I was destroyed." Charlie handed the map to Max.

"I have a map, too," added Adam, "that's what we've been using."

Charlie and Max studied the three maps because they wanted to see if all the maps were the same.

"Looks like these are all identical," confirmed Max.

"I wonder how many maps are out there? If we have three copies, there might be hundreds circulating and numerous people looking for the same mountain. Once we get there it could be emptied," remarked Lucy.

As everyone got up to follow Max and Charlie in the direction of Mine Mountain, Steve continued to read a book.

"Steve, what are you doing?" asked Kyra.

"I wanted to read about Mine Mountain in this book Avery the Librarian gave me. Maybe it could help us," Steve said as he held up the book.

"This is no time to read," complained Henry. "We have to keep moving."

"But it says here that Mine Mountain keeps regenerating diamonds, so there will be diamonds when we find it," Steve informed them as he read from the book. "So we should still look for the mountain."

"Look!" Owen called out and began to sprint.

"Watch out!" warned Lucy, "I see a cactus. Don't get too close."

The gang ran toward Owen. They spotted a desert well and stopped beside it.

"I knew it!" Owen was excited. "A desert well. I've never seen one of these before. It's amazing." Owen looked down at the blocks of sandstone that formed beside a deep blue patch of water.

Kyra inspected the well and asked, "What does it do?"

Owen stared at the well. "I'm not sure. I think it can help us get water."

Henry peered into the well and exclaimed, "Guys, there's a stronghold underneath the well. Let's go inside!"

Steve was reluctant to go into the stronghold. "I don't mind going into the stronghold. I just don't want to go to the End. I don't have the energy to beat the Ender Dragon."

It was too late. Nobody had heard Steve. Everyone had already climbed down into the well and made their way into the stronghold.

"Look at this fantastic room!" Owen said as he walked into a room with a pillar and a large fountain.

"Watch out!" Steve screamed as a grayish bug with black eyes crawled toward Owen.

Max hurried toward the bug and struck it twice with his sword. "Silverfish," said Max, "we have to be on the lookout. They usually spawn in strongholds; there could be a lot of bugs crawling around this stronghold."

"You're right," Lucy's voice quavered, "Look!"

A horde of gray silverfish crawled across the sandy floor, surrounding the group. Owen hopped up on the pillar to avoid an attack.

"What should we do?" Kyra had her sword out and struck a couple of silverfish but more crawled into the room.

Henry took out a block of TNT.

"What are you doing?" Kyra asked. She didn't want to explode.

"We have to walk along the pillar and make it to the spiral staircase. Once we're upstairs, I'll ignite the TNT," Henry informed them.

Owen had already made his way toward the stairs, striking as many silverfish as he could along the way from the pillar.

"A silverfish bit me!" Kyra called out as she hit the small insects with her diamond sword while trying to reach the safety of the stairs.

"Don't worry. I have some potions that will help restore your health," Adam reassured Kyra as they tried to remain calm during the short and rather intense trek to the spiral staircase.

Once they had all reached the staircase and walked downstairs and into a large library, Henry ignited the TNT and blew up the fountain room.

Kaboom!

The explosion rocked the room. Henry inspected what remained of the fountain room. "It looks like we were able to destroy all of those silverfish. Let's hope the spawner was destroyed. I don't want another insect invasion."

Kyra explored the stronghold's library. "I wonder if there are any more books on Mine Mountain in this library," she said as she looked at the dusty shelves filled with leather books. Cobwebs and chests lined the room. The group looked at the books on the shelves.

Henry called out, "Guys, come in here! I found a storeroom with a bunch of chests."

The gang headed toward the storeroom filled with chests. Each person had his or her own chest to open.

"It feels like my birthday," Lucy said excitedly as she opened her chest. "I wonder what's in here."

Lucy's chest was filled with enchanted books. The group crowded around her and examined the books.

"These are excellent. We can use these to enchant swords," Steve said, looking at the books.

"Open your chest, Steve," said Lucy.

Steve carefully opened his chest. It was filled with apples. "We should eat these now." Steve shared the apples with his friends.

As the gang devoured the tasty fruit, the others opened their chests. The chests were filled with everything from iron pickaxes to gold ingots. Everyone shared their items, although Beatrice and Charlie didn't think this was the best idea.

"Why do we have to share everything?" questioned Charlie.

"Because we're in this adventure together," replied Max.

As they distributed the loot and placed it in their inventories, Steve looked at all of these useful treasures and said, "This is incredible!"

"And you were the one who didn't want to go into the stronghold," remarked Henry.

"I just didn't want to go to the End," Steve defended himself.

"Speaking of the End, how are we going to get out of here?" asked Kyra. "Do we have to travel to the End to get out?"

Kaboom!

"What was that?" asked Charlie.

"Maybe somebody else is here and is trying to defeat the silverfish?"

"Or maybe it's a creeper!" Lucy cried out as a green creeper crept into the storeroom.

Chapter 9
IN THE DISTANCE

"We have to get out of here!" Lucy called out to the group.

"Where should we go?" Owen had never been in a stronghold and had no idea how they could escape.

"Quick, I see another staircase," Henry said as the group hurried away from the creeper.

Max turned back and struck the creeper with an arrow and it exploded. The gang raced down the stairs only to find a bedrock wall at the bottom.

"We're trapped," Owen panicked.

"We need to light torches so hostile mobs won't spawn. It's too dark in this stronghold," Lucy told the group. They lit torches and placed them on the walls of the stronghold.

"We should use our pickaxes to dig a hole out of here," Steve instructed them.

The gang took out their new pickaxes and began to bang against the wall of the storeroom but their efforts didn't even make a dent.

"I think it's all bedrock underneath here," Steve observed, looking at the wall.

"Let's move to another part of the stronghold," said Henry, and the group left the storeroom and found themselves in a jail.

"I wonder who they kept in this creepy jail?" Lucy asked as she placed a torch on the wall. She didn't want to turn this into a jail full of hostile mobs.

The light from the torches didn't stop a silverfish from crawling too close to Lucy's leg.

"A silverfish!" Max lunged at the bug, striking it twice.

"We have to get out of here before we deal with another silverfish infestation." Steve sprinted down the hallway but stopped when he saw a creeper lurking at the end of the hall.

Max shot an arrow at the creeper and it exploded.

"We have to keep moving," said Steve. "There has to be a way out of this stronghold."

They kept close together as they explored the cavernous stronghold with its many rooms. Soon they reached another jail. Owen opened the door to the jail.

"What are you doing?" Beatrice questioned Owen. "We don't want to get trapped in there!"

"Look, more silverfish." Henry struck the two small insects. "They are so hard to see because they blend into the wall."

"This place is a death trap. We have to escape," Kyra said nervously as she looked for a wall that might be easy to break through. There didn't seem to be a logical exit; they were walking through an endless series of rooms, as if they were caught in a puzzle.

"I think this is the End room." Henry stood by a room with an Ender Portal.

"I am not going to the End," Steve said defiantly.

Charlie and Beatrice took out their pickaxes. At first Steve thought they were about to threaten him with the pickaxes but they didn't. The two of them banged the pickaxes against the wall.

"We made a hole!" Charlie called out.

"The wall isn't made of bedrock!" Beatrice said as she hit the pickaxe against the wall.

"We don't have to go to the End," Steve said in relief.

The rest of the group took out their pickaxes and banged them against the wall, and within minutes they saw light.

"The desert!" Kyra cried out, "I was never so happy to see a sandy desert!"

One by one they crawled through the hole in the wall and onto the sandstone blocks.

"Just when we thought we were safe," Max remarked as the sun began to set, making the group vulnerable to attacks from hostile mobs.

"We have to light some torches," said Lucy as the sun set quickly.

A group of zombies lumbered toward the gang.

"After the battle in the stronghold, this will be easy," Henry said, and he charged at the zombies.

"Don't be too confident," Kyra warned him, "this won't be as easy as we think. Everyone has a low health bar."

Two zombies reached for Lucy. Max jumped in front of them and struck them with his sword.

"Guys, we have to have our swords out at all times. We can't let these zombies defeat us. We are too close to Mine Mountain to be destroyed!" Max said as he raced toward a group of zombies.

"Do you think somebody is spawning them to stop us from reaching the mountain?" asked Kyra, while striking a zombie.

"It could be the work of a griefer or it could just be a zombie attack. This is when they spawn," Steve said as he clobbered a group of zombies.

"At this point, we have to stop talking about why the zombies are here and just get rid of them," added Henry.

As the zombie battle intensified, the group tried to strike as many zombies as they could with their diamond swords. Adam threw a splash potion of weakness on the zombies, and the gang was able to defeat the dead mobs.

After the zombies were defeated, Adam said, "Since this is another sleepless night, we need to drink potions to regain strength."

The zombie battle must have taken longer than the gang had realized because within in a few minutes the sun was rising.

"We're safe!" Kyra said happily.

"I see trees in the distance," remarked Henry.

Max studied the map. "It's just past this forest. We are almost there!"

The group ran toward the trees. As they approached the forest, a wolf raced past them.

"Ignore it," said Henry, "we need to focus and find Mine Mountain. We are almost there."

"Nothing is stopping us," Beatrice told them. "We are mining for diamonds before nightfall."

An arrow flew at the group. They looked around but didn't see anyone.

"It can't be a skeleton," said a very confused Steve. "It's too light out."

"Let's keep moving," Max directed as he looked at the map. "Mine Mountain is right here."

Another arrow flew through the sky and struck Charlie. "I've been hit," Charlie called out in pain.

"Are you okay?" asked Beatrice.

Meanwhile, Max noticed something nearby. "It's Mine Mountain. I see the entrance," exclaimed Max.

"How are we going to get in?" Kyra wondered, as five rainbow griefers stood in front of the entrance. The rainbow griefers aimed their bows and arrows at the gang.

Chapter 10
DIAMONDS IN THE DARK

The gang rushed toward the rainbow griefers with their diamond swords. But the battle was hard. The griefers had a lot of energy and were well supplied.

"Why are you doing this to us?" shouted Steve. "There are enough diamonds for everybody. And we've traveled so far."

The griefers didn't reply with words. They just shot more arrows and struck the gang with their powerful swords.

Adam tossed a potion of weakness on the griefers and then splashed a potion of invisibility on himself and his friends.

"Come on, we have to be quiet so they can't find us," whispered Adam. He and his invisible friends made their way into the legendary diamond mine.

The group couldn't see each other, so they weren't aware that they all stopped at the same time and stood in awe at the entrance of Mine Mountain. The walls had a bluish glow. The floor of the mine was filled with layers of diamonds shining through the ground.

"This is incredible," remarked Lucy.

"Shh!" Kyra reminded Lucy, "we don't want the griefers finding us."

Lucy looked back. "But I don't see the griefers. They must still feel the effects from Adam's potion."

"Still, we don't want to draw attention to ourselves. That wouldn't be good," Kyra told her friend.

The gang hiked farther into the mine and began to mine for diamonds. If somebody else had walked into the mine right then, they might have let out a chuckle. They would see pickaxes digging into the ground, but they wouldn't see a person holding them. It almost looked like ghosts were mining for diamonds in this mythical mine.

As Kyra mined she looked down and could see her hand. "We're not invisible anymore." Kyra looked over and saw her friends beside her, mining for diamonds.

The group continued to mine and gather diamonds. "I think I have enough diamonds to create armor for everyone," Steve announced. As he mined deep within the ground, he started to think about Thomas. He knew that he would need these valuable diamonds to help rebuild his village. Steve hoped Thomas wasn't causing any problems while he was gone.

"How many diamonds do we need?" asked Kyra. "I think I have enough."

The group began to count the many diamonds they had mined. When four green forms lurked in a corner of the mine, Steve noticed them and called out, "Watch out for the creepers!"

Kaboom! One exploded near Charlie and destroyed him.

"No!" shouted Beatrice as she shot an arrow at another creeper, destroying it.

The others battled the creepers but they were a challenge to fight. If they got too close, you were a goner.

"Why are all of these creepers here?" asked Kyra when they finally got a break.

Beatrice paced. "Where was the last place Charlie slept?" She couldn't remember. She wanted to get back to her friend.

"I'm sure Charlie and Cyrus will meet up and find us," Owen reassured Beatrice.

Three more creepers appeared from the shadows as the gang sprinted from the mine. When they reached the exit, four rainbow griefers holding diamond swords attacked them.

"Looks like you aren't invisible anymore," one of the rainbow griefers taunted the gang.

"Drop the diamonds now!" a griefer demanded.

"No!" shouted Kyra as she struck the griefer with her sword.

"If you drop the diamonds, we won't attack you," a griefer said calmly.

Steve was shocked to see Henry drop his diamonds. Steve didn't trust these griefers. The others followed Henry and dropped them. The griefers picked up the gang's diamonds.

"What about your diamonds?" A particularly colorful rainbow griefer questioned Steve.

Steve placed them on the ground. The griefer smiled at Steve then said, "This is the end for you." He ran toward Steve with a diamond sword.

"Liars! I knew you'd still attack!" Steve screamed as he fought back, striking the rainbow griefer with his sword, but the griefer wasn't destroyed and was able to hit Steve again. Steve's energy bar was running low. He was worried that he might not be able to fight anymore.

"Look at that!" Steve pointed at a group of rainbow griefers descending from the mountain that housed the diamond mine.

"Oh my!" Lucy looked at the griefers advancing toward them. "Adam, do you have potion that could get us out of this?"

Adam took a gulp of the potion of invisibility and sprinted around the griefers, throwing various harmful potions on the griefers that were battling his friends. Each time a griefer was splashed, he'd let out a cry. They weren't sure who was splashing them and they wanted it to stop. Adam also knew that when his potion wore out, he'd be in trouble. With a few seconds left, Adam splashed as many rainbow griefers as he could, but it wasn't making a serious impact. They needed more help.

Arrows flew at the rainbow griefers. They looked over to see Charlie and Cyrus, dressed in armor and ready to battle the griefers.

"Charlie!" Beatrice shouted, happy to see her friend.

"This is no time for reunions," Henry said looking at Beatrice. "Pay attention, we have to clobber these rainbow griefers."

One of the griefers lit a brick of TNT and threw it at Steve and his friends. The gang jumped back, just missing the powerful explosion. The gang raced toward the mountain, trying to escape the griefers, but the sun was beginning to set and Steve noticed the creepers slowly emerging from the mountain.

"It looks like there's an army of creepers." Lucy was shocked. Unlike other hostile mobs that often traveled in packs, she had never seen that many creepers together before.

"If they all ignite at once, there is no chance we'll survive." Henry shot arrows at the creepers.

"Why did you shoot arrows?" Max said angrily. "Now they know where we are. We have to get out of here."

"But where can we go?" Lucy asked as she followed Max far away from the diamond mine.

"Now we don't have any diamonds. We need to go back to the mine." Steve was upset. He needed these diamonds. He was worried about the fate of his village and the damage Thomas might have caused while he was away.

The group sprinted faster. Steve could barely keep up. His energy was low. They reached the water.

"Where can we go now? Should I build a boat?" asked Kyra.

Adam passed out the potion for water breathing.

"We'll stay under the water until dawn. It's our only chance for survival," Adam said as he took a gulp of the potion and dove into the deep blue ocean.

Chapter 11
OCEAN MONUMENT

"More creepers!" Lucy called out, as a hoard of green explosive beasts floated silently toward the group.

Everyone drank the potion of water breathing and dove in after Adam. When they were deep beneath the ocean's surface, they spotted their friend. A blue one-eyed fish with orange spikes swam past the group. Its tail moved quickly.

"It's a Guardian!" Steve shouted to his friends, "and it's ready to attack."

"There must be an ocean monument nearby," Henry said. He tried to swim as fast as he could but wasn't quick enough. The Guardian shot a laser at Henry, striking him.

"Ouch!" Henry called out and his movements slowed rapidly. "I can't move."

"It's mining fatigue," Max told him as he skillfully shot an arrow that destroyed the fish.

Lucy swam to collect the prismarine crystal the fish had dropped in the water, and then moved toward Henry. "How are you?"

"A little better." The mining fatigue faded but it had depleted Henry's energy bar. He had barely enough energy to follow his friends.

"We need to swim deeper. I think I see something," Lucy stated and she swam toward an ocean monument. As they approached the mammoth underwater temple lit by sea lanterns, a guardian shot a purple laser at the gang. The laser turned to yellow as the group tried to swim away from the powerful healing beam that saved Henry.

Max took out his arrow and aimed toward the fish.

"Don't shoot, this is a good fish. He just shot a healing laser," Henry called out to his friend.

An Elder Guardian swam by the entrance to the ocean monument. Max shot an arrow, striking the sea creature but didn't destroy it.

"We need to shoot more arrows," Max informed his friends.

Arrows shot through the water. Max shot the final arrow. Before succumbing to Max's arrow, the Elder Guardian was able to shoot one last laser. The yellow laser hit Kyra and she was instantly struck with mining fatigue.

"Her health bar is too low," Henry said as he swam toward Kyra. "If she's attacked one more time, she'll be destroyed."

Adam looked through his inventory of potions. "I don't have any potions that could help you regain your strength," he told her.

"Would milk help?" Lucy asked as she found some milk in her inventory.

Kyra drank the milk, which gave her enough energy to enter the ocean monument.

Inside the temple, the gang swam through the many chambers, as they kept an eye for both Guardians and Elder Guardians that might be swimming through this underwater temple.

"Every ocean monument has three Elder Guardians," explained Steve, "so we have to watch for the remaining two that are guarding this place."

"I think we just found number two." Just as Lucy spoke these words, the purple laser struck her from the Elder Guardian. When the laser turned a yellowish color, she was hit with mining fatigue.

The Elder Guardian shot a laser at Max. He tried to swim away from the laser beam but it was too late, he was hit.

Charlie and Beatrice shot arrows at the Elder Guardian, destroying it. Max drank some milk to recover from the mining fatigue.

"I know there is a room with gold." Beatrice swam around the temple in search of treasure and told the gang, "I've been in one of these temples before and walked away with a lot of loot."

"Watch out!" warned Steve. The final Elder Guardian appeared, shot a laser at Beatrice, and then swam toward her. The gray fish with blue thorns hit Beatrice.

"Ouch!" she screeched from the thorny bump. Beatrice couldn't escape. Max shot arrows at the beast, but he couldn't save Beatrice.

"Oh no!" Kyra called out as Beatrice disappeared.

"This is awful," Charlie moaned. He was devastated. He had just been destroyed recently and he knew how hard it was to get back to the others. He didn't think they'd see Beatrice for a long time and there was no way she'd make it back to Mine Mountain. The trip was too dangerous to do alone. They were barely surviving even though they had a large group for backup.

Henry and Max flooded the sea creature with arrows, trying to destroy this rather strong spiky fish.

"It's so powerful," Max said as he let out an exhausted sigh. "I don't feel like we can destroy it."

"We can! We just have to keep shooting arrows," replied Henry.

The fish was infuriated and charged toward Henry and Max, ready to attack them with its spikes.

Lucy and Kyra swam behind the fish and hit it with their diamond swords. Wagging its tail, the fish swam straight toward Henry and struck him with a blue spike.

Lucy shot an arrow at the fish. After being struck with several arrows, the fish was weakened. The Elder Guardian tried to attack Henry again, but before it could hit him with its dangerous fatal spikes, the fish was destroyed.

The group raced around the ocean monument in search of treasure.

"I found it!" Lucy shouted as she swam into a room filled with gold.

"Maybe we don't have any diamonds, but we'll definitely have some gold." Henry placed gold in his inventory, as the rest of the group gathered gold bricks.

"Isn't this nice," a voice boomed through the room.

"Yes, I love a happy ending," another voice shouted and then let out a laugh.

Two rainbow griefers stood in the doorway.

Max shot an arrow but it missed them. One rainbow griefer called out, "This is a losing battle. We have the entire ocean monument filled. Now give us your gold."

"Never!" Steve screamed. He was about to swim toward the griefer with his diamond sword, when he heard a growling noise.

A Guardian swam behind the griefers and struck them with its laser, destroying the griefers.

Max and the others shot a flood of arrows at the Guardian.

The gang swam out of the room filled with gold, searching the temple for other rainbow griefers.

"Those two griefers said this temple was full of griefers," Max said as he swam past a series of empty rooms.

"Would you trust a griefer?" asked Steve.

"I think our potion is wearing out," Adam gasped for breath, "we have to make it to the surface."

The gang swam out of the temple and toward land. When they finally reached the surface, they couldn't believe who was standing in front of them.

Chapter 12
THE MORE THE MERRIER

"Thomas," Adam stood on the shore and stared at his old friend in disbelief. "How did you find us here?"

"I didn't know you were here," replied Thomas. "I was exploring. I'm just as shocked to see you."

Steve emerged from the water. "Thomas," Steve questioned, "why are you here?"

Although Steve was glad Thomas was standing in front of him and not destroying his town like he had imagined, he wondered if Thomas had something to do with the rainbow griefers. It seemed too much of a coincidence that he was here on his own.

"I was exploring," Thomas said while he watched the others reach the surface of the water and walk onto the shore. "Wow, I can't believe all of you are here."

"Do you seriously think we believe you?" Adam asked Thomas.

"What are you talking about?" Thomas stuttered.

"You want us to believe that you were just exploring when you found us coming out of the water?" Adam was upset.

"Especially since we were just attacked by rainbow griefers?" added Steve.

"Well, um . . ." Thomas couldn't get the words out.

"Admit it, Thomas. You are griefing again." Adam took out his sword and walked toward Thomas. "How can you do this?"

"I never said I was griefing," Thomas defended himself and backed away.

"Well, we all find it suspicious that you are standing by the water." Lucy also took out her diamond sword, advancing toward Thomas.

"Please don't attack me," Thomas cried. "I'm innocent."

"Prove it!" Kyra stood in front of Thomas with her diamond sword.

"How?" Thomas asked.

"We're about to head back to Mine Mountain. I'm sure we'll see some rainbow griefers there. If they know who you are—" Adam called out, but Thomas interrupted him.

"They won't. I have no idea what you're talking about," Thomas pleaded.

Two arrows flew through the air.

"Rainbow griefers!" Charlie screamed, "I can see them. Get ready to battle them."

Thomas took out his bow and arrow and was ready to fight alongside Adam.

"Thomas!" One of the rainbow griefers screamed as Thomas shot an arrow at him, "What are you doing?"

"I knew it," Adam turned and pointed his diamond sword at Thomas, "I knew you were guilty. Why would you lie to us?"

"No," Thomas confessed, "I'm lying to the rainbow griefers. I want to help you."

Adam was confused. He didn't know whom to believe. But there wasn't time to contemplate whether Thomas was innocent because a group of rainbow griefers sprinted toward them. Adam fought them with his diamond sword and didn't turn back to see if Thomas followed him.

Clang! Bang! Adam was struck by a rainbow griefer's sword. Max snuck up behind the griefer, helping Adam with this skilled griefer. Although the griefers were strong fighters, they were seriously outnumbered by Steve and his friends and within minutes the gang had defeated this small group of rainbow griefers.

Yet there was no time to take a breather, as more griefers were approaching. Steve and his friends were worried, but Adam had a plan to destroy them all.

Adam called out to his friends, "Guys, come here!"

The gang sprinted toward Adam and formed a circle around him to hear his plan. Thomas joined the circle but Adam stared at him and said quite coldly, "I'm sorry, but you don't belong here."

Thomas took out his sword and rushed toward the griefers that were making their way toward Steve and the gang. Adam didn't know if Thomas was planning on attacking the griefers or joining them, and he didn't care. Adam had a plan.

"When the griefers approach, I'm going to splash my potion of invisibility on them and us. We have to stick together as a group and run away once I splash the potion on them. They won't realize we are gone and will wind up shooting at each other, and they'll destroy themselves," Adam told them as he held the potion of invisibility in his hand.

"But there might be one griefer left," suggested Max.

"Then we'll outnumber him and it will be an easy fight," replied Adam.

"That's an amazing plan," remarked Lucy.

Six griefers surged toward them. "I see you guys just standing there ready to surrender," one of the griefers yelled.

"Never!" Steve screamed.

Adam splashed everyone with the potion of invisibility.

"I can't see anything!" one of the griefers cried out.

Arrows shot through the sky. People were struck. As the potion wore off, Steve and his friends were the only ones remaining except for one rainbow griefer, who threw a block of TNT at them and then ran away.

"Jump!" Steve yelled, but it was too late and Charlie and Owen were caught in the explosion.

"Oh no, we lost Charlie and Owen," cried Lucy.

"And Thomas," added Adam.

The group was tired. The sun was beginning to set. They wanted to find a place to spend the night.

"I wish I was at my wheat farm. I want to sleep in my bed," Steve groaned as night fell and the group were left vulnerable in an unfamiliar part of the Overworld.

"There's no point in complaining, Steve." Kyra was annoyed. "We all want to go to sleep, but we can't."

Adam surprised everyone. "I don't want to sleep. I want to figure out a plan to get rid of these rainbow griefers. If we just stop fighting for one minute and sit down and think of a plan, we can probably defeat these menaces."

The group agreed. They needed to find a plan. They also needed to fight the creepers that slowly floated in their direction.

Arrows flew through the air as the creepers exploded. The gang saw two skeletons walk past.

"Let's hide," suggested Kyra quietly.

"No, let's dig!" said Steve, as he dug his pickaxe into the ground.

"What are you doing?" asked Lucy.

"I'm making a hole for us to hide in. We only have to go three blocks down; we can jump in and stay there until morning." Steve had already dug a deep hole and jumped in.

Using their last bits of energy, the group dug holes in the ground to seek shelter for the night and to hide from the bony skeletons.

"I hope we'll be safe here," Lucy remarked as they stood close to each other in the hole.

"We'll be fine," Adam said and drank a potion.

"What are you drinking?" asked Kyra.

"It's a potion for night vision," replied Adam. "I'll keep a lookout for us."

Adam peeked out of the hole. "It looks like we are fine. There's nothing out there."

Kaboom!

"Adam, what was that?" Kyra was nervous.

Adam paused and stared off into the distance. He didn't say anything.

Chapter 13
FIERY BATTLE

Four yellow blazes flew by with two white ghasts trailing behind them. Thomas sprinted through the dark night and was struck by a fireball from the blaze.

"Someone's summoned a blaze and ghasts," Adam shouted. He saw Thomas disappear within the smoke.

"Someone?" Lucy was annoyed. "You mean the rainbow griefers."

"I'm sure you're right. And I saw Thomas get hit by a fireball," Adam said.

"Thomas? I thought he was destroyed," said Steve.

"He must have respawned," Adam replied while he looked out from the hole.

"I think you should stop peeking out of the hole, we don't want one of the blazes or ghasts to see you," warned Kyra.

Steve could see the sun rising. "It's almost morning, we can get out."

"The blazes and ghasts were summoned. They are only supposed to be in the Nether, which means even if it's daylight, they could still attack us," Henry said as he too, peeked over the hole.

"We have to battle these fiery mobs from the Nether or we'll never get back to Mine Mountain." Steve was ready for battle.

Although he was ready to battle, he was also distracted. He couldn't stop thinking about Thomas. He wondered why he was sprinting through the Overworld at night. He wondered why he was alone. He wondered where Thomas would respawn now that he was destroyed again. These thoughts spun around in his head as he heard Lucy cry, "Watch out!"

First there was a high-pitched scream and then they saw the fireball. Steve narrowly avoided the blast from the ghast. He didn't have time to shoot the fireball but attempted to deflect it.

Max used the hole to hide from the floating flamethrowers and shot arrows.

"Bull's-eye!" Max called out as he destroyed one ghast.

"One down," added Lucy as she aimed for whatever hostile mob flew past them.

The blaze flew close to the gang and shot a fireball at the hole. They quickly jumped to safety.

As the gang fought hard, a person appeared in the distance.

"It's Thomas," said Kyra. "What should we do? Should I shoot him with an arrow?"

"No, we have to find out why he keeps coming over here. And he must be respawning very close by. Maybe he can lead us to the rainbow griefers," said Steve.

Max hit the final ghast with its own fireball. "Gotcha!"

"Good job, Max," Lucy smiled.

As the large yellow creatures with black eyes circled above them, the group worried that it was just a matter of time before they were destroyed by a blaze's fireball.

"We have to get rid of these blazes or it will be raining fire soon," Lucy warned them.

"I'm trying," replied Max, as he aimed at the blaze.

"Stop attacking them," Steve told Max.

Max was confused and he put his bow and arrow down. "What should we do?"

"Just sit. If we stop attacking them, I think they'll leave us alone." Steve hoped what he said was true.

The group stood silently by the large hole. The blazes began to lower themselves from the sky and land on the ground.

"No, let's sprint," Steve instructed his friends and they followed closely behind him.

When they reached the dense forest, Steve stopped. "We need to eat something. I see a chicken."

"I'll hunt it," said Max.

"And I'll prepare the meal," Lucy offered because she loved to cook.

The group feasted on the chicken and then Thomas approached them.

"This is no time to rest," Thomas warned. "The rainbow griefers have summoned more blazes and ghasts. There's no way you'll survive."

"It seems that we've already survived the first attack," said Max, "you were the one who was defeated."

"I was coming here to warn you," explained Thomas. "I was shocked that the ghasts and blazes had already been summoned."

"Are they also summoning the creepers?" asked Lucy.

"I'm not sure. I just know it's not safe here and you guys should head home," replied Thomas.

"We know it isn't safe," said Kyra," but we aren't going home. We are going to Mine Mountain and we're going to get the diamonds."

"I think the rainbow griefers are intimidated by us," remarked Steve.

"The rainbow griefers scared and bothered by you? That's funny," Thomas laughed.

"If they weren't, they wouldn't use such drastic tactics. They don't need to summon beasts from the Nether; they could battle us with their swords. But they see what skilled fighters we are and they know they can't beat us without using dirty tricks." Steve was upset. He had enough of griefers. They were always ruining everything in the Overworld.

"Why are you here?" Lucy didn't understand Thomas and spoke honestly. "You tell us that you want to help, but then you defend the griefers. What is your problem?"

"I do want to help you but—" Thomas tried to get the words out but Steve didn't want to hear it.

"Stop! We don't care. Just go back to the rainbow griefers. We can't trust you," Steve shouted.

"You don't have to trust me. But I'm running low on resources and my energy bar is almost empty. If you give me a piece of chicken, I will tell you what the rainbow griefers are planning," begged Thomas.

Lucy handed him a piece of chicken. "I'm only giving this to you because you're hungry. Don't bother giving us any tips. We won't believe you anyway."

Thomas blurted out, "But I know their plan. They are going to summon the blazes and ghasts by the entrance to Mine Mountain. If you are able to defeat the blazes and ghasts, once you enter Mine Mountain, they're going to throw blocks of TNT in the mine and blow you guys up."

"We need to destroy the rainbow griefers before they attack us," Steve remarked.

Henry paused and then asked, "Where do they sleep?"

"They sleep in a cave not very far from here."

"Lead us to the cave," demanded Henry.

Chapter 14
BURNING DOWN THE HOUSE

Thomas led them to a cave deep within the forest, with an entrance hidden by leaves. Steve looked for rainbow griefers that could be lurking outside the dwelling.

"Shh!" Lucy said, "I can hear voices."

There was a low hum coming from inside. Steve and the others stood by the entrance and tried to listen but they couldn't hear what the rainbow griefers were saying. Meanwhile Henry was taking blocks of TNT from his inventory.

"I wonder what they'll think when they get a taste of their own medicine?" Henry ignited the TNT and threw it into the entrance.

Kaboom!

The griefers' headquarters went up in flames.

"Run!" shouted Henry and the group ran toward Mine Mountain.

Arrows flew at them as they rushed past the enormous trees that filled the lush forest. Max shot arrows back at the two griefers who survived the blast and were chasing them. "I got them!" Max exclaimed when the griefers were destroyed.

"I wonder where they'll respawn," remarked Steve, "they have no home now."

The gang continued to sprint through the forest.

"I see it!" Lucy called out. "I see Mine Mountain."

"We need to keep watch and make sure the sky doesn't fill with ghasts and blazes," Lucy said as they entered Mine Mountain.

They were still in awe of the bluish glow from the diamond-filled mine but they couldn't stop and take in the breathtaking sight. They needed to mine for diamonds as quickly as they could.

"Thomas, why are you still here?" asked Lucy.

Thomas dug his pickaxe into the ground and began to mine. "I just helped you destroy the rainbow griefers' house. Can't you see I'm on your side?"

"I don't know what you're planning, Thomas. But I still don't trust you." Adam dug deep within the ground. He placed diamonds in his inventory.

"I just want to mine for diamonds. I'm not planning anything," Thomas said as he held his pickaxe.

"You can mine with us, but when we are ready to leave, you must go your own way," Steve told Thomas. Steve thought it was a fair compromise.

Lucy added, "Yes, we don't want you coming with us and leading us into a trap."

The group gathered the diamonds, placed them safely in their inventory, and then exited the mine.

"Wow, that was easier than I thought it would be," said Kyra.

"Famous last words," Henry said as he looked up at the sky filled with ghasts and blazes.

The gang rushed back into the mine, when Lucy let out a shrill scream. "Creepers!"

Creepers floated by the wall of the mine. Max shot an arrow at a creeper but the explosion almost destroyed everyone in the mine.

"We can't destroy creepers in this mine. It's not big enough," Lucy said. She had barely survived the blast from the creeper.

The gang hurried toward the exit as a fireball landed at their feet.

"Is everyone okay?" Henry asked, while shooting an arrow into the sky. He hoped he would hit something.

"There's nowhere to hide," Steve said, admitting he was terrified. "Wherever we go, somebody is trying to blow us up!"

"Not if they can't see us," Adam said. He reached for his potion of invisibility but realized the bottle was empty.

Thomas took a snowball from his inventory and threw it at the ghasts and blazes. "Shoot the creeper!" he yelled at Max. Max hit the creeper and it exploded.

"Here," Thomas handed Max snowballs. "I need you to throw these while I get something."

Then Thomas took out a potion of invisibility and splashed it on them.

"Now run!" Thomas screamed.

The group didn't know which direction they should run but they knew they had to get out of there fast. They sprinted through the forest and into the jungle. They hoped when the potion wore off they would be able to find each other.

Chapter 15
CREEPERS OR CREEPS?

When Steve became visible, all he could see were leaves. He had run into the forest. A wolf raced past him. Steve walked on a grassy path lined with oak and birch trees, searching for his friends, but he couldn't find them. He called out their names, but there was no response.

The sun was beginning to set and Steve began to craft a cabin for the night. It was a very quick build, nothing fancy, but there was a bed and he'd have shelter for the night. When he had completed the cabin, he heard some rustling in the distance. Steve took out his diamond sword and placed a torch on the outside of his newly built cabin. He walked slowly into the dense forest to find out who was lurking outside his home.

With his diamond sword out and ready for action, Steve pounced at the person or hostile mob that was hiding behind a tree.

"Stop!" the voice called out.

"Thomas!" Steve said angrily, "what are you doing here?"

"I don't have any place to go," replied Thomas.

"Do you know where the others are?" Steve questioned.

"No, I don't," Thomas said as he pointed out a creeper in the distance. "This forest isn't safe. In fact the whole area around Mine Mountain isn't safe. It's infested with creepers."

Steve saw an arrow fly past them and straight at the creeper.

"Who shot that?" Steve called out, but there was no reply.

"Let's go to your house," suggested Thomas.

"Who said you can take shelter in my house?" Steve was annoyed that Thomas assumed he could stay at the house.

"There is no time to argue," Thomas said as he saw another creeper. "This forest has too many creepers and it's very dark. I can't see anything. If we don't go back to your house now, it might be too dark to find it."

Another arrow shot through the sky and destroyed the creeper as Steve walked toward the house with Thomas. "I wonder who is shooting these arrows?" he questioned.

Thomas replied, "I have no idea but I don't have the energy to fight them if they start shooting at us."

Steve approached the front door of the small cabin and told Thomas, "I don't have a bed for you."

"That's okay, I can craft one," replied Thomas.

The two entered the house, and Thomas began to craft a bed for himself.

"When you said the forest and the area around Mine Mountain are infested with creepers, do you know if the rainbow griefers are the ones infesting the area? Do they have a creeper spawner?"

"No, I don't think they are involved. This is one of those areas that happens to have a lot of creepers."

Steve took out one of the books he had gotten from Avery the Librarian and began to read about the area around Mine Mountain. Maybe Thomas was telling the truth and this was simply a challenging part of the Overworld. Steve flipped through the pages and couldn't find any reference to creepers. As he drifted off to sleep, he tried to keep one eye open but couldn't. He didn't trust Thomas.

Within seconds of falling asleep, Steve heard someone at the door. "Who is it?" Steve got out of bed.

"Don't just ask who is it," Thomas replied irritably, "they could be here to attack us."

"If anyone is attacking us, it's your friends, the rainbow griefers."

"I told you, I'm on your side now," Thomas shouted.

Wearing diamond armor and holding his powerful sword, Steve opened the door slowly.

"Steve!" Lucy smiled. She was standing in the doorway with Kyra.

"Can we come in?" asked Kyra.

"We are being chased by creepers. Max, Henry, and Adam have been shooting arrows at the creepers all night," Lucy informed Steve.

"So that is who was shooting the arrows!" Steve was glad that they were friends and not foes.

Lucy and Kyra entered the small cabin. There was barely enough room for them to stand and there certainly wasn't enough room to construct two more beds.

"Help!" a voice called out from the forest.

"It's Max!" cried Kyra. "We need to get our armor on and help him battle the creepers."

The group rushed out of the cabin. Steve's jaw dropped when he saw the sea of green between the leaves. As creepers exploded, more spawned. They were in the midst of a creeper invasion.

"Are you sure there isn't a spawner in this jungle?" Steve asked Thomas as they walked into the middle of this fiery battle.

"I don't think so, but I'm not certain," admitted Thomas.

"Well, we have to find out," Steve said as he shot arrows at creepers and watched a bunch of mini explosions light up the dark night sky like fireworks.

Steve and Thomas ran toward Henry, Max, and Adam but on the way there they fell into a hole in the ground.

"What is this?" Steve looked around.

"It looks like a stronghold." Thomas walked over to a staircase as a creeper emerged from a corner. He aimed at it and destroyed it. Thomas walked down the stairs and said, "Steve, I think there is a spawner and it's here."

Steve followed Thomas but couldn't find him. "Thomas," he called out.

"Help!" He could hear Thomas struggling.

Steve ran down the hall. He found Thomas locked in a jail cell in the stronghold.

"How did you get in there?" asked Steve.

Thomas didn't have a chance to reply. Cyrus and Owen were standing with their diamonds swords aimed at Steve.

"Give us all your diamonds," Owen demanded.

Chapter 16
TROUBLE'S BREWING

"Why are you doing this?" Steve asked them.

"It's very simple. We want all the diamonds for ourselves," Cyrus replied.

"What about Beatrice and Charlie?" asked Steve.

"They'll take care of your friends." Owen laughed.

Thomas had already destroyed a cave spider. They were trapped in the small cell, while Cyrus and Owen were spawning creepers just a few feet from them.

"Steve!" Lucy called out.

"Don't come down here, it's a trap," Steve cried from behind the bars of the small jail cell.

Although Steve warned Lucy to stay away from the stronghold, she hurried down the hall toward the jail cell. She wanted to save her friend.

"Lucy, stop!" Steve called out, but it was too late. Cyrus and Owen demanded she hand over all of her diamonds and forced Lucy into the small jail cell beside Steve and Thomas.

"We have to warn the others," Lucy said, because she was worried about Kyra, Max, Henry, and Adam.

Owen counted the diamonds. "Don't worry about them. I'm sure Beatrice and Charlie have destroyed them by now."

Cyrus spawned more creepers and added, "Or maybe the creepers got to them before Beatrice and Charlie."

"Nobody destroyed us," Henry said as he and Adam ran past the jail cell and shot an arrow at Owen and Cyrus.

Adam splashed a potion of harming on the two sinister diamond thieves. "You're the ones who are going to be destroyed."

Kyra breathlessly rushed into the stronghold and called out, "Henry! Are you here? Beatrice and Charlie are destroyed!"

Kyra paused when she saw her two friends behind bars. "What are you doing here?"

"Let us out," Steve shook the bars. "We need to help Henry and Adam destroy the creeper spawner."

"And we need to defeat Owen and Cyrus," added Lucy.

Kyra opened the door to the jail. "Owen and Cyrus?" she asked. Kyra was confused.

"Yes, they are behind this whole creeper invasion," Steve remarked. "They are working with Beatrice and Charlie."

"They're diamond thieves," added Lucy, as they all sprinted toward the creeper spawner, ready to deactivate it.

Steve and his friends reached the creeper spawner. They approached the spawner and could see Cyrus battling Henry while Adam cautiously tried to deactivate the spawner without exploding himself.

Max shot an arrow at Cyrus, destroying him.

"Good shot," exclaimed Henry.

"He stole our diamonds!" Lucy shouted. "Get them from him."

Max grabbed the diamonds Owen had dropped and handed them to Lucy.

"These are for Steve and Thomas." She handed them the diamonds and they thanked her.

"I'm glad we have the diamonds back but we have to stop this spawner!" shouted Adam.

Thomas grabbed three torches from his inventory and placed them by the spawner to stop any creepers from spawning from the black cage.

Henry held a brick of TNT. "We have to blow this place up and we're going to need a lot of TNT."

The others grabbed TNT from their inventories. They placed the TNT by the spawner, ignited it, and sprinted as fast as they could to safety.

When the gang emerged, it was daylight and the sun was shining brightly. There were no rainbow griefers in sight and everyone felt at peace.

"Now that we all have our diamonds, we should head back home," suggested Steve.

"Great," Kyra looked over at Steve, "I'll head back to the wheat farm with you."

"We're not going back to the wheat farm, we are planning to go on a treasure hunt," said Lucy. "Now that we have all of these diamonds, we can make great armor to protect ourselves and go on an extreme treasure hunt!"

Everyone was ready to part ways until Kyra shrieked, "Ouch!"

Arrows shot through the sky striking Henry and Max. The battle wasn't over.

Chapter 17
REWARDS

"Get your bows and arrows out," Henry said as he tried to figure out where the arrows were coming from and who was attacking them.

"Do you see rainbow men?" asked Adam.

"No, I can't see anything because of the leaves," replied Henry.

Steve looked up and saw Charlie and Beatrice in a tree and they had their bows pointing at the group.

"Look up!" Steve enjoined the group.

Henry and Max aimed for Charlie and Beatrice but missed.

"They must have a house near here because they respawned very quickly," noted Steve.

"We have to defeat them. We don't want them stealing our diamonds." Lucy was determined to win. She shot another arrow at Beatrice and Charlie.

A lone yellow blaze flew through the air, taking note of the two people perched in the green oak tree, and let out a fiery blast. Beatrice and Charlie barely had enough time to move, when the fireball hit them.

Max aimed at the yellow blaze and shot an arrow. The others copied Max and shot at the floating flamethrower until it was erased from the sky.

"Finally!" exclaimed Lucy. "We have to get out of here."

"Not so fast," a familiar voice called out.

"We aren't afraid of you, Owen," Lucy said as she sprinted toward him with her sword. But Cyrus threw a splash potion on Lucy that weakened her.

"Lucy!" Kyra rushed to her friend's side as Owen splashed a potion of harming all over Kyra.

Max charged at Owen with his sword. With three hard blows he defeated the evil villain and then helped Lucy and Kyra by giving them milk.

Henry battled Cyrus. It was a tough battle. Cyrus was a skilled fighter. Their diamond swords clanged as the fight intensified.

"You'll never win!" Henry told him, "Evil never does."

"Ha!" exclaimed Cyrus. "You're wrong, Henry!"

Max and Adam crept up behind Cyrus. Max struck Cyrus with his sword and Adam threw a potion of weakness on him.

"No, you're wrong, Cyrus!" Henry said, delivering the final blow and wiping out the sinister Cyrus.

Steve looked around and didn't see any hostile mobs that were summoned to attack them, or any colorful griefers. In fact, he just saw trees and sunshine. "I think we're safe, but we better get out of here before they return."

"Yes, we have no idea where they will respawn," added Lucy.

The gang hurried out of the forest and into the familiar sandy biome. The sun was beating down on them and they were hungry.

"Do you think it's safe to stop and eat now?" Kyra asked, looking behind her. She wanted to make sure their old enemies weren't planning an attack.

The group stopped and rested. They needed energy for their journey away from Mine Mountain.

"I still can't believe we went to Mine Mountain." Steve was shocked they actually made it to the famed mountain and had filled their inventory with a huge supply of diamonds.

"I know!" said Kyra. "Everyone back home will be so excited to hear our stories."

"We should write a book," suggested Steve. "Avery can keep it at the library."

"That's a great idea," Kyra smiled.

Lucy had a chicken in her inventory and cooked it. She handed out portions of chicken and even gave some to Thomas. The group stopped feasting when they heard voices nearby.

"It sounds like Beatrice and Charlie," remarked Lucy.

The group hid behind a tree. They could hear Beatrice and Charlie talking to each other.

"I can't believe we don't have any diamonds. We should go back to Mine Mountain," Charlie complained.

"We can't, the rainbow griefers will attack us with blazes and ghasts. It's too hard," said Beatrice.

"But Steve and his friends were able to get the diamonds," Charlie told her.

"Our only hope was getting the diamonds from them, but it's too late. We will try to go back to Mine Mountain another time," explained Beatrice.

"Or maybe Cyrus and Owen can get them from Adam's house," plotted Charlie.

Steve was about to jump in front of both of them and strike them with his diamond sword but Henry held him back.

In a whisper Henry said, "Let them go. We've fought enough. They'll just get destroyed and respawn, but they'll never learn anything."

Steve realized Henry was right. Charlie and Beatrice were the ones who were walking away empty-handed. If they battled them, it would just be a waste of time. Steve looked through his inventory and was excited to see the many diamonds that filled it. He knew when he went home he'd be able to trade them and use them to help his village thrive.

Chapter 18
SHARING IS CARING

"Are you going to go back to your town?" Kyra asked Adam.

"I'm not sure," replied Adam.

"How can you even consider going back there? Didn't you hear Charlie and Beatrice plotting to steal your diamonds with Owen and Cyrus?" asked Lucy.

"Yes, I heard it." Adam was confused. He liked his new town and didn't want to move because some criminals threatened to steal his diamonds. But he also missed having trustworthy neighbors like Kyra and Steve.

"You can come and stay with me until you figure out where you want to live," suggested Kyra.

"That's very nice of you," Adam said. He was happy to have such a good friend. "But I'm not sure I want to go back to your village."

"Is it because of everything I did?" asked Thomas.

"Well," Adam stuttered, "it's not all because of that, but—"

Thomas interrupted, "I'm going to go back to the village. I want everyone to see how much I've changed. And when I get back to the village, I'm going to give up my diamonds to the people who live there. I was a menace there and I think giving up these diamonds is a great way to repay everyone."

"You're going to give up all of your diamonds?" Lucy was shocked. They had worked so hard for those diamonds. Yes, Thomas did cause a lot of trouble but giving up all of his treasure was a real sacrifice.

"I think that's a great idea," said Steve.

"Thanks." Thomas smiled.

"If you want," Steve told him, "you can stay with me in my house."

"I can stay with you?" Thomas was both surprised and happy.

"Yes," Steve looked at Thomas, "I trust you."

Thomas was excited to return to the village.

Kyra said, "Well, Steve it looks like we have our old neighbors back."

"Yes, we do," replied Steve and then he looked at Henry, Lucy, and Max. "Is there any way we can convince you to come back to the village with us?"

Henry paused and then replied, "We'd love to, but we have our hearts set on an ultimate adventure."

"Yes, it's going to be epic," added Max.

"We're going to build a house underwater and hunt for treasure from ocean monuments." Lucy was excited as she talked about their plan.

Adam walked over to them and handed them bottles of potions. "This will help you with your treasure hunt. It's the potion for water breathing."

"Thanks!" Henry was thrilled since this was an extremely useful gift.

"When you're done with your underwater treasure hunt, please come visit me on the wheat farm," said Steve.

"We will," Lucy said as a goodbye.

Steve was sad to say goodbye to Lucy, Henry, and Max.

As the group parted ways, Steve, Kyra, Thomas, and Adam walked along the water while Lucy, Henry, and Max drank the potion and dove into the deep blue ocean. Steve and Kyra looked back to see their friends, but they were already deep under the sea.

Steve and Kyra were happy to be heading back to town with lots of diamonds and some old friends.

The End

DO YOU LIKE FICTION FOR MINECRAFTERS?

Check out other unofficial Minecrafter adventures from Sky Pony Press!

Invasion of the Overworld
MARK CHEVERTON

Battle for the Nether
MARK CHEVERTON

Confronting the Dragon
MARK CHEVERTON

Trouble in Zombie-town
MARK CHEVERTON

The Quest for the Diamond Sword
WINTER MORGAN

The Mystery of the Griefer's Mark
WINTER MORGAN

The Endermen Invasion
WINTER MORGAN

Treasure Hunters in Trouble
WINTER MORGAN

SKY PONY PRESS

Available wherever books are sold!